The Bunnies' Counting Book

Written and illustrated by Elizabeth B. Rodger

A GOLDEN BOOK • NEW YORK

Western Publishing Company, Inc., Racine, Wisconsin 53404

© 1991 Elizabeth B. Rodger. All rights reserved. Printed in the U.S.A. No part of this book may be reproduced or copied in any form without written permission from the publisher. All trademarks are the property of Western Publishing Company, Inc. Library of Congress Catalog Card Number: 90-84667 ISBN: 0-307-00203-9
MCMXCIII

Sally is the littlest bunny. She is one bunny. Just Sally by herself makes one. She has one lollipop and one pink hat.

Can you count one of anything else?

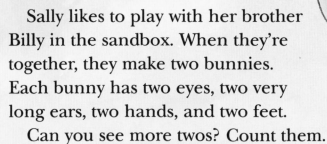

Sally likes to play with her brother Billy in the sandbox. When they're together, they make two bunnies. Each bunny has two eyes, two very long ears, two hands, and two feet.

Can you see more twos? Count them.

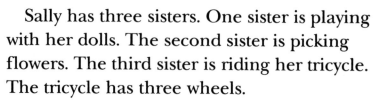

3
three

Sally has three sisters. One sister is playing with her dolls. The second sister is picking flowers. The third sister is riding her tricycle. The tricycle has three wheels.

Can you see more threes? Count them.

Sally has four brothers. Three brothers and Billy make four. Billy can kick the ball very hard for a little bunny. Well done, Billy! He has scored a goal.

4
four

5
five

Oh, dear! This time Billy has kicked the ball too hard. It is lost in the sunflower patch.

Can you count five beautiful sunflowers?

"Scat! Get out of here!"
Billy rushes out of the
sunflower patch followed
by six angry mice. The
little mice were taking a
nap in the sunflower
patch.

7
seven

Seven bunnies play follow-the-leader.
"All together, hop-hop-hop," says the first bunny.

But one hungry brother has stopped to have a snack.

Can you count the number of carrots he is going to eat?
Did you say seven?

Good for you!

8
eight

Four brothers and four sisters make eight bunnies playing on a jungle gym. The bigger children can climb high. Sally, the littlest bunny, has fun swinging on the lowest bar.

The bunnies hear their mother calling. She has wonderful news. They are going on a picnic. Lots of aunts, uncles, and cousins will be there.

There are nine bunnies now. Eight children and one mother make nine.

10
ten

Father Bunny is packing ten bottles of raspberry juice in the picnic basket. Can you count the tens of anything else?

What fun! What excitement! Ten bunnies
set off for a picnic.
Can you count the bunnies?

Ten bunnies walk up a hill on their way to the picnic.

Here come Grandma and Grandpa Bunny. Grandma makes eleven bunnies. Grandpa makes twelve.

But wait! Here comes Uncle Fred whizzing along
on his bike. He makes thirteen bunnies.

He has just passed Uncle Sam and Aunt Polly,
carrying a large cooler filled with goodies. They make
fourteen and fifteen bunnies.

Now there are fifteen bunnies going to the picnic.

The fifteen bunnies walk down the other side of the hill on their way to the picnic.

Look! Can you see five cousins running over the hill? Fifteen and five make twenty—sixteen, seventeen, eighteen, nineteen, twenty.

Now there are twenty bunnies going to the picnic.

20
twenty

The twenty bunnies reach the picnic spot. There is lots of delicious-looking food to feed all those hungry bunnies.

But look! Here come more aunts, uncles, and cousins. Now there are thirty, forty, fifty bunnies at the picnic! Will there be enough food for everyone?

50
fifty

What a sight! What
skipping and hopping as
the young bunnies play
game after game.

There are so many bunnies
having fun at the picnic.

After a long day, it is time to go home.
Lots of happy, yet tired bunnies wave
good-bye—except Sally, the littlest bunny,
who is sound asleep.